WORK
AND PLAY

Written by Sydnie Meltzer Kleinhenz • Illustrated by Mick Reasor

Children's Press®
A Division of Scholastic Inc.
New York • Toronto • London • Auckland • Sydney
Mexico City • New Delhi • Hong Kong
Danbury, Connecticut

Dear Parents/Educators,

Welcome to Rookie Ready to Learn. Each Rookie Reader in this series includes additional age-appropriate Let's Learn Together activity pages that help your young child to be better prepared when starting school.

Work and Play offers opportunities for you and your child to talk about the important social/emotional skill of **natural curiosity**.

Here are early-learning skills you and your child will encounter in the *Work and Play* Let's Learn Together pages:

• Opposites
• Number recognition
• Making associations

We hope you enjoy sharing this delightful, enhanced reading experience with your early learner.

Library of Congress Cataloging-in-Publication Data

Meltzer Kleinhenz, Sydnie.
 Work and play/written by Sydnie Meltzer Kleinhenz ; illustrated by Mick Reasor.
  p. cm. — (Rookie ready to learn)

 Summary: A girl looks at different jobs as she thinks about what she might do someday. Includes learning activities, parent tips, and word list.
  ISBN 978-0-531-27179-7 (library binding) — ISBN 978-0-531-26829-2 (pbk.)

 [1. Stories in rhyme. 2. Occupations--Fiction.] I. Reasor, Mick, ill. II. Title.

 PZ8.3.K675Wo 2011   [E]—dc22   2011010397

Acknowledgments
© 2005 Mick Reasor, front and back cover illustrations, pages 3, 5, 7, 9, 11, 13, 15, 17, 19, 21, 24–29, 30 police officer, 31–32. Page 27: © Getty Images/Thinkstock, Hemera/Thinkstock.

1 2 3 4 5 6 7 8 9 10 R 18 17 16 15 14 13 12 11

People work in inside places.

3

People work in outside spaces.

People work in morning light.

People work in dark at night.

9

People work above the street.

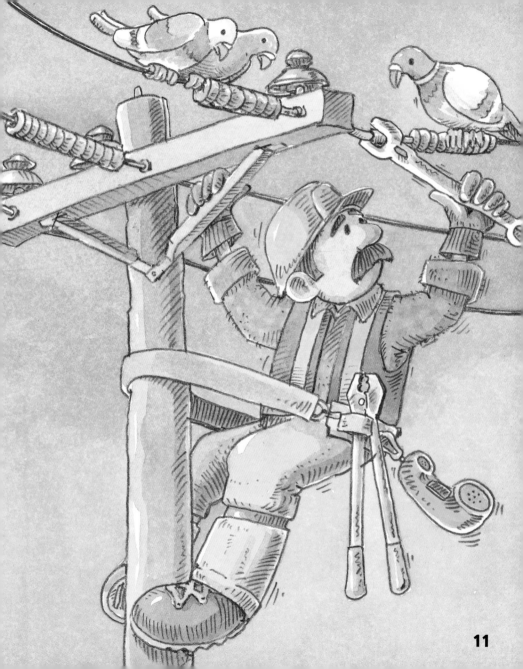

People work below my feet.

People work in cold or heat.

People work to buy or sell.

I have work I do as well.

19

Are things I do at school
and play...

like work that I may do someday?

Congratulations!

You just finished reading *Work and Play* and learned about the many helpers who work in your community.

About the Author

Sydnie Meltzer Kleinhenz is Mom to five boys and a girl dog. When she plays, she racewalks at a park or goes dancing. When she works, she teaches fourth graders in Houston, Texas, where the things they do at school and play might be the work they do someday.

About the Illustrator

Mick Reasor is an artist, a teacher, a husband, and the father of four brilliant girls. He lives, works, and plays in Grand Rapids, Minnesota.

Work and Play

Let's learn together!

Community Helpers

(Sing this song to the tune of "Skip to My Lou.")

Community helpers
around us we see
Making our neighborhood
a fun place to be.

Police keep us safe
for work and play.
Mail carriers bring
us letters each day.

Bakers sell food
oh so yummy.
Freshly made rolls
fill my tummy!

So many jobs, so much to do.
Which special workers have
helped you?

PARENT TIP: Share this song to help your child learn about different community helpers. Then go back through the story and have your child identify the different community helpers he sees. Ask: "What kind of work would you like to do when you grow up? Why?"

What's the Opposite?

Some people work inside. Some people work outside. "Inside" and "outside" are opposites.

Say each word in the top row. Then point to the word that is its opposite in the bottom row.

empty   **up**   **hot**

down   **cold**   **full**

PARENT TIP: As your child matches the opposites in the pictures above, be sure to emphasize the label words to build language and word-recognition skills. Then go back through the story and ask your child to find pictures of other opposites, such as *hot* and *cold* weather, *daytime* and *nighttime*, and *above* and *below* ground.

27

Cool Tools!

Many people work in our community.
Each community helper needs the right tools to do the job.

- Point to what the painter needs to finish painting the ceiling.
- Point to what the baker needs to finish making a pie.
- Point to what the mail carrier needs to carry his letters.
- Name what the lifeguard uses.

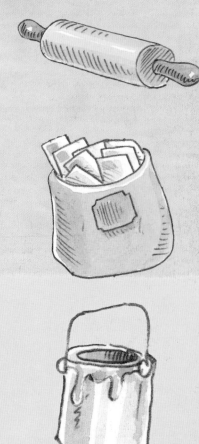

PARENT TIP: As you enjoy this matching activity together, help your child build language skills by naming the community helpers and their tools. Then ask your child to find other community helpers, and the tools they use to do their work, in the story.

29

Here, Kitty Kitty!

After the police officer found the dog, she had to search for a lost cat. Help her find the cat. Use your finger to follow the pictures that rhyme with [cat].

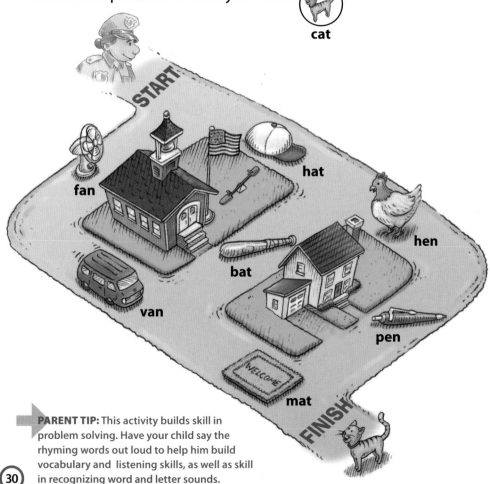

cat

START

fan

hat

hen

bat

van

pen

WELCOME

mat

FINISH

PARENT TIP: This activity builds skill in problem solving. Have your child say the rhyming words out loud to help him build vocabulary and listening skills, as well as skill in recognizing word and letter sounds.

How Much Does It Cost?

Look at the price on each fruit in this picture. Then point to the correct number on the chart that shows how much each fruit costs.

	banana	5¢	10¢
	pear	15¢	20¢
	watermelon	10¢	20¢

PARENT TIP: Your child will be building object/number recognition, as well as language skills, as you enjoy this activity. Help your child identify each fruit, as well as the prices, as he matches the foods in this picture to the correct prices below.

Work and Play Word List (38 Words)

above	I	play	that
and	in	school	the
are	inside	sell	things
as	light	someday	to
at	like	spaces	well
below	may	street	work
buy	morning		
cold	my		
dark	night		
do	or		
feet	outside		
have	people		
heat	places		

PARENT TIPS:

For Older Children or Readers:
Go through the story and help your child identify the word *people* each time it appears. Then have him find the word *people* on the word list. Talk with your child about the people he is familiar with, and the work they do, in your own community.

For Younger Children:
Point to and share the word *night* on the word list with your child. Then go back through the story together. See if she can find the nighttime scene in the story. Ask: "What do you like best about nighttime?"